THE DIARY OF A SHORT, STOCKY, BALDING, ARAB MAN

Written By

Mark Rabahi

First published 2026 by AtomicMonday

ISBN 978-1-7646825-0-3 (EPUB)
ISBN 978-1-7646825-1-0 (PDF)
ISBN 978-1-7646825-2-7 (Paperback)
ISBN 978-1-7646825-3-4 (Hardback)

For Dad.

And Ruby.

These entries blend lived moments, imagined
scenarios, and emotional extrapolations.

They are presented, unashamedly, in screenplay form.

Diary Entries

1
"84 Weeks"

INT. WOOLWORTHS SELF-SERVICE CHECK OUT — NIGHT

Mark, our titular short, stocky, balding, Arab man, scans his items through the self-service check out.

The supermarket is quiet. Mark is the only one at the check out.

The self-service attendant, Janet (20s, brunette, piercing eyes) sidles over to Mark's terminal and stands guard.

Packet of chips. Beep. Block of chocolate. Beep. Jar of Nutella. Beep. Coffee Big M. Beep.

Mark self consciously looks over his shoulder as he's scanning and spots Janet.

She gives him a look. Half wince. Half pity. Half disgust.

> **MARK**
> When the pregnant wife has cravings, you know?

Janet softens. She nods her head approvingly.

> **JANET**
> You're a good husband!

> **MARK**
> Oh, I should have said fiancé. We're waiting for the little one to arrive first.

> **JANET**
> Sorry, I didn't mean to pry.

> **MARK**
> No that's quite alright.

Bag of M&Ms. Beep. Bag of Party Mix. Beep.

> **JANET**
> Those cravings are something else, aren't they?

> **MARK**
> One night it's choccies, the other it's exclusively a savoury world.

Janet laughs.

                        JANET
         How far along is she?

Beat. Mark smacks his lips.

                        MARK
         Oh it'd be about 84 weeks now.

Beat. Both Janet and Mark do some mental math. Janet is faster.

                        JANET
         84 weeks? She's been pregnant almost 2 -

                        MARK
         - I just mean it feels that long! She's at 34 weeks. Any day now!

                        JANET
                   (matter of factly)
         Well --

Mark pays with his phone. He collects his shopping bag.

                        MARK
         See ya, darl.

                        JANET
         All the best!

INT. MARK'S HOUSE — LATER

Mark sits on his couch watching TV in a dark room. He eats a fistful of M&M's. A fistful of chips. A drink of a Big M. A spoonful of ice cream. He pops a can of Pepsi Max. He takes a deep, pained breath.

INT. MARK'S BATHROOM — LATER

Mark looks at himself in the mirror.

                        MARK
         You fucking piece of shit.

                                                        END

2

"1 Million by Paco Rabanne"

EXT. THE WOOD FIRE PIZZA PLACE — DAY

Mark, our titular short, stocky, balding, Arab man, sits across from Dion (tall, dark, handsome, flowy hair).

They eat their respective meals.

Mark cuts a big piece of his schnitzel and impales it with his fork.

He looks over at their waitress, Arianna (20s, slim, wavy hair).

> MARK
>
> Do you think the waitress likes me?

> DION
>
> I can't have this conversation again.

> MARK
>
> I did the manners, the smile, I asked her what she'd recommend, I know they love that, but I'm sensing this coldness.

> DION
>
> Listen, every time we come here -

> MARK
>
> - We don't come here a lot -

> DION
>
> - I've worked in hospitality. Yeah? The turnover is high. She won't be here forever.

> MARK
>
> Why don't I ever consider the turnover? I'm a fucking idiot that's why.

> DION
>
> If you're going to make a move, I suggest you do it soon.

> MARK
>
> You're right, you're right. I know you're right.

Arianna notices Mark looking at her. She makes her way toward the table.

MARK

Oh fuck.

Mark bites the big piece of schnitzel off his fork. He chews rapidly as she approaches.

Dion nonchalantly sips his water.

Arianna sidles up to the table.

ARIANNA
(beaming)

How is everything?

DION

Yeah, great, thanks.

Mark forces down his food. Painfully.

MARK

Really good, thank you.

Arianna looks at Mark. She smiles.

ARIANNA

You smell really good.

A smile forms on Mark's face.

MARK

Oh?

ARIANNA

Yeah, that's really really nice. What is that?

Mark looks at Dion. Dion looks at Arianna. Arianna looks at Mark. Mark's eyes widen. He gathers himself.

MARK

1 Million by Paco Rabanne. Not many people know about it.

ARIANNA

I love it!

Arianna pulls out her phone and Googles it.

Mark and Dion look at each other, elated.

ARIANNA

Oh yep, found it.

MARK

Glad I could oblige.

ARIANNA

Yeah, I'm definitely going to buy it for my boyfriend. Thanks!

Arianna leaves the table.

Beat.

END

3

"The Waiter"

INT. THE RESTAURANT — NIGHT

Mark, our titular short, stocky, balding, Arab man, sits across from Stacey (blonde, rosy cheeks).

                    STACEY
          Thanks so much for asking me.

                    MARK
          Thanks for saying yes.

Their eyes lock. Dual smiles.

Their waiter, Brandon (tall, dark, handsome), approaches the table.

                    BRANDON
          Hiya.

Mark and Stacey break their eye contact and turn to Brandon.

                    BRANDON
          Can I start you off with some drinks?

Mark reaches for the drinks menu.

                    MARK
          Let's have a squiz.

                    STACEY
          Do you guys do an espresso martini?

                    BRANDON
          We sure do, Sassafras.

Mark shuts the menu.

Stacey blushes.

                    STACEY
          One of those please.

                    BRANDON
          You got it.

Brandon turns to Mark.

BRANDON

You?

MARK

Pepsi Max please.

BRANDON

We don't have Pepsi Max. If you open that one back up to the kids menu you'll see our soft drinks.

MARK

Just a water thanks -

BRANDON

- Water, got it.

Brandon smiles at Stacey. He leaves the table.

INT. THE RESTAURANT — NIGHT

Mark and Stacey enjoy their meals.

MARK

And then, he straps his couch to his roof and drives home using a broom and a rope to control the car!

STACEY
(feigning enthusiasm)

Oh my.

MARK

You've really never seen Mr Bean?

STACEY

I really haven't.

MARK

I find that absolutely incredible.

Stacey looks across the restaurant and catches Brandon's attention.

She smiles and playfully turns her head to the side. She points at her empty martini glass. Brandon winks at her.

Mark winces.

INT. THE RESTAURANT — NIGHT

Mark and Stacey have cleared their plates. Mostly. Mark's plate still has his fresh, green salad.

Brandon approaches the table.

BRANDON
I'll clear those.

Brandon begins collecting the plates.

BRANDON
Didn't want your salad, big man?

Mark starts to speak. He stops.

Stacey chuckles.

Mark sits there. Fuming. His rage escalating. His anger reaching previously unknown bounds.

STACEY
Thanks.

Brandon leaves.

Beat. Long beat.

MARK
I can't be with someone who hasn't watched Mr Bean.

Mark throws his napkin on the table.

He gets up and leaves.

END

4

"Emotions"

INT. MARK'S HOUSE — NIGHT

Mark, our titular short, stocky, balding, Arab man, sits on his couch, immersed in his TV show.

The more he watches, the more he begins to crack.

He becomes more and more overcome with emotion.

He forcefully wipes away tears as they begin to form.

A weep escapes his fragile body.

He takes a few deep breaths and composes himself.

He shakes his head.

We change focus to the TV. Mark is watching an episode of Everybody Loves Raymond.

END

5

"The Good Kind of Arab"

INT. THE WORKPLACE — DAY

Mark, our titular short, stocky, balding, Arab man, sits around a round table with colleagues Nathan (glasses, white) and Amanda (blonde hair, whiter).

> **AMANDA**
>
> Not to mention the protests!

> **NATHAN**
>
> The protests are the fucking worst!

> **AMANDA**
>
> Like, I'm trying to get my shit from Mecca and I have to contend with all these gypsy sympathisers.

Mark sips his coffee.

> **NATHAN**
>
> They're gypsies, the Palestinians?

> **AMANDA**
>
> I thought the protesters were Aboriginal?

> **NATHAN**
>
> I don't know if you're allowed to call Aboriginals, gypsies.

> **AMANDA**
>
> That's another thing, people trying to police speech. If I want to call an Aboriginal a gypsy, I'm going to fucking do it. Freedom of speech.

> **NATHAN**
>
> Amen, sister. We used to be a country!

> **AMANDA**
>
> Too many pinko-liberal soft dicks in power. They've really ruined this country.

Mark sips his coffee.

> **NATHAN**
>
> We need guns.

> AMANDA

Absolutely -- oh! The protesters were Palestinians.

> NATHAN

Oh?

> AMANDA

Yeah. I remember all the watermelons.

> NATHAN

If they have it their way it'll be Sharia Law here in Melbourne.

> AMANDA

I swear, if Islam is so good then go practice it in your own country, dogs.

> NATHAN

They don't even have a country.

> AMANDA

It's honestly pathetic. Poor Israel, surrounded by all those Islamic countries. What're they supposed to do? Let themselves be overrun by barbarians?

> NATHAN

You really get it, you know?

> AMANDA

It's just like, did we learn nothing from 9/11? Keep the Quran out of the country, that's what I say.

Amanda looks at Mark. She bites her tongue.

> AMANDA

Oh -- sorry.

> NATHAN

Don't worry about him, he's one of the good Arabs. Christian.

> AMANDA

Good for you, mate. All things are possible through Jesus.

NATHAN

Fucking-A.

Mark sips his coffee.

END

6
"The Rowville Rapist"

EXT. SUBURBAN STREET — NIGHT

Mark, our titular short, stocky, balding, Arab man, walks, head down, AirPods in, along a deserted suburban street.

A few paces ahead of him is Eloise (red hair, dark features).

Eloise crosses the street.

A moment later, Mark crosses the street. He nods along to the music in his AirPods.

Eloise looks behind her, she notices Mark.

After a few paces, she takes a left down a street.

She looks behind her, and after a few paces, Mark turns down the same street.

She begins to look worried.

They continue walking, Mark remaining a few paces behind.

Eloise turns into another street.

After a moment, Mark follows suit.

Eloise takes a deep breath. She fights the tears away.

She turns around.

ELOISE

Stop following me!

Mark, AirPods in, head down, doesn't notice, and keeps walking.

ELOISE

Help! Someone help me!

Mark gets close enough to notice Eloise screaming. He removes his AirPods.

MARK

Are you okay?

ELOISE

Stop following me!

MARK

Follow -- what?

ELOISE

You've been following me for the last 10 minutes and I'm sick of it!

MARK

I'm sorry I was just heading home -

ELOISE

- You're him, aren't you?

MARK

What?

ELOISE

The Rowville Rapist. You're fucking him I knew it.

MARK

I'm not the Rowville Rapist. I'm no raper. I haven't even done a single rape.

ELOISE

Look at you. Textbook rapist build. Can't get a girl so he forces them. Well not today, mister!

Mark tries to walk past Eloise. She thinks he's trying to grope her.

ELOISE

I said no!

Mark starts crying. Hard.

Eloise winces.

ELOISE

What the fuck?

The crying doesn't stop. Mark collapses to the floor. Crying.

Eloise maintains her disgust.

ELOISE

Rapist fuck.

Eloise walks away. Mark weeps.

END

7
"Blind"

INT. THE COFFEE SHOP — DAY

Mark, our titular short, stocky, balding, Arab man, sits alone at an empty table.

He taps his fingers rapidly on the smooth wood.

He checks the time on his phone.

He looks up at the entrance.

He wipes sweat off his brow.

The waiter, Jason (Polynesian, warm) approaches the table.

JASON

Ready to order?

MARK

Still waiting on someone.

JASON

No worries, fella. Give me a shout when you're ready.

Jason leaves the table.

Mark begins texting on his phone.

Cassandra (cute) enters the coffee shop.

She looks around the shop and spots Mark.

She reviews a photo of him on her phone, and then him at the table again.

She sighs the familiar sigh of disappointment.

She approaches his table.

Mark looks up and notices Cassandra.

He puts his phone away. Smiles.

END

8
"Number 4"

INT. THE BARBER SHOP — DAY

Mark, our titular short, stocky, balding, Arab man, sits in a barber chair.

Jay (21, tall) gracefully airs out the apron and ties it around his neck.

Mark avoids looking directly at the mirror, his own reflection unbearable.

Jay quizzically looks at Mark's scruffy but short hair.

> **JAY**
> What're we doing today, chief?

Mark glances at the mirror to see his hair, and then looks away.

> **MARK**
> The usual, I guess.

> **JAY**
> Number 4?

> **MARK**
> Sure.

Jay prepares the clippers and begins trimming Mark's hair.

> **JAY**
> How you been? Good?

Mark sighs.

> **MARK**
> Living the dream, man.

> **JAY**
> How's work? Good?

> **MARK**
> Yeah very good.

> **JAY**
> Got a girlfriend? She good?

                              MARK
          Yeah. Good.

                              JAY
          Fucken nice, mate.

Every stroke of Jay's clippers reveal Mark's hairline receding deeper and deeper up his head.

Mark sneaks glances at himself in the mirror.

Jay cleans up the sides.

                              JAY
          Bit of hair down the neck.

Mark exhales.

                              MARK
          Yeah a bit. Thanks.

Jay cleans up the neck.

Jay blow dries the apron and removes it.

                              MARK
                           (to himself)
          Fuck.

The apron is removed, and Mark is met face-to-face with his newly shaved head atop his rotund body.

He is utterly disgusted.

Jay holds up the mirror to show Mark the back of his head.

                              JAY
          Good?

                              MARK
                           (quietly)
          I'd like to kill myself.

JAY

What's that?

MARK

Yeah it looks good. Good.

Jay smiles. He playfully pats Mark on the shoulder.

JAY

Mel Gibson in the 80's, mate.

Mark sighs.

END

9
"Wee Wee Wee All The Way Home"

INT. THE VEHICLE — NIGHT

Mark, our titular short, stocky, balding, Arab man, finds himself miraculously wrapped in a heated embrace with Lane (30s, Irish, spunky).

They separate, both wearing a satisfied grin.

                    LANE
          You're an animal.

                    MARK
          Sorry.

                    LANE
          No I fucking love it.

                    MARK
          Oh.

                    LANE
          I have a question.

                    MARK
          I have an answer.

Beat. Lane buries a cringe.

                    LANE
          Can you --

Lane smiles, embarrassed. Her cheeks turning a crimson red.

                    MARK
          Yeah?

                    LANE
          Can you -- I want you to put a finger in.

Mark's next word catches in his throat.

He takes a breath.

                              MARK
          Okey dokey.

They share an intense look.

They inch closer and closer.

Mark raises his hand.

                              MARK
          Which one?

Lane is slightly taken aback.

                              LANE
          What?

                              MARK
          Which finger would you like?

                              LANE
          I, um --

                              MARK
          The thumb may have access issues, right? Though it does offer the
          claw manoeuvre.

Lane, puzzled, shakes her head.

                              MARK
          Index and middle could work well as a two-in-one combo.

A smile returns to Lane's face. She nods.

                              LANE
          Now we're -

                              MARK
          - Nails are a bit long. Just give me a --

Mark starts biting away at his nails.

Gnawing like a rodent. Spitting.

Lane is disgusted. She shakes her head.

> **MARK**
> What? Trust me you don't want the ring finger it completely lacks any dexterity or purposefulness. It's a decoy finger. Like Pippen in game six.

Lane is drying up faster than the Sahara at midday.

> **LANE**
> Okay.

> **MARK**
> And obviously we can't use the pinky.

Long beat. Lane's curiosity gets the better of her.

> **LANE**
> Why?

> **MARK**
> Because the pinky goes wee wee wee all the way home.

Beat. Long beat. Lane exhales.

> **LANE**
> Give me the claw manoeuvre.

END

10
"UNO"

INT. THE GYM — MORNING

Lane walks slowly, but purposefully, on a treadmill in a busy gym.

Sydney (20s, buxom) walks on the treadmill beside her.

> SYDNEY
>
> Where did you say you met him?

> LANE
>
> Caribbean Gardens.

> SYDNEY
>
> Why are we trawling markets for men, now?

> LANE
>
> I'm a fiend for antiques, don't be a bitch.

> SYDNEY
>
> Did you find anything? Other than a man?

> LANE
>
> He's not my "man". And yeah I found a deck of UNO cards from the 80s it's pretty sweet we should totally play.

> SYDNEY
>
> Yeah we'll definitely do that. Fucking insane or what?

> LANE
>
> Suddenly you're too good for UNO?

> SYDNEY
>
> It feels like we're veering. Are we veering?

> LANE
>
> There's a veer.

> SYDNEY
>
> What was his name?

> LANE
>
> Mark.

                    SYDNEY
Where's he from?

                     LANE
Rowville.

                    SYDNEY
Rowville. Please tell me you're not dating the Rowville Rapist.

                     LANE
I'm 99% sure he is not the Rowville Rapist. But who knows. My
first celebrity.

                    SYDNEY
Fucking hell. Is he hot?

                     LANE
Next question.

                    SYDNEY
You and stray dogs.

                     LANE
He's not a dog!

                    SYDNEY
But he has doggish qualities -

                     LANE
- There's a doggishness.

                    SYDNEY
Tall?

                     LANE
Not particularly.

                    SYDNEY
Fit?

                     LANE
Maybe once.

SYDNEY

Solid head of hair though right?

LANE

Next question.

SYDNEY

This cunt must be Hamish and Andy levels of funny then.

LANE
(cringing)

Hamish and Andy?

SYDNEY

Fuck off.

LANE

You ever hear of the claw manoeuvre?

SYDNEY

Is that a joke?

LANE

No but it is a bit uncomfortable.

SYDNEY

What're you doing?

LANE

He just seems nice.

SYDNEY

Nice.

LANE

Yeah nice. Is there a problem with that?

SYDNEY

I suppose not. Me, I need --

Sydney thinks better of it. She trails off.

SYDNEY
Nice.

Beat.

They walk side by side.

SYDNEY
Tell me about the claw.

END

11
"Why Are You The Way That You Are?"

INT. MARK'S HOUSE — NIGHT

Mark, our titular short, stocky, balding, Arab man, sits on his couch, scrolling on his phone.

He is on Lane's Instagram profile, scrolling meticulously through her photos.

Lane at work. Lane at the bar with friends. Lane's family.

Mark continues to scroll, as he does, the timestamp on the photos get further and further into the past.

Lane with her dog. Lane with a man. Lane standing in front of a SOLD sign.

Mark scrolls. His curiosity intensifying.

Lane on New Years Eve. Lane eating a pizza.

Lane on the beach in a skimpy bikini.

Marks's eyes widen. He examines the photo. The sand. The ocean. The bikini top.

He tries to zoom in. His fingers, seemingly with a mind of their own, instead double-tap the screen.

The red heart, indicating a like, appears on screen, mortifying him beyond belief.

His eyes bulge. He notices the date of the image: "January 23, 2014". Beads of sweat appear on his forehead.

He quickly unlikes the image and locks his phone.

He takes a deep breath.

He reaches for his phone in a panic and begins Googling with the ferocity of a man who's life hangs in the balance.

He searches:

"Do Instagram likes always give a notification?"

"Do Instagram likes do notification 2026?"

"Instagram like notification quickly unlike?"

"Fuck you're a fucking idiot."

"I hate you. I hate you."

"Does Instagram notify of likes from a picture over 10 years old?"

Mark's face turning redder and redder.

INT. LANE'S HOUSE — NIGHT

Lane's phone lights up with an Instagram notification.

Lane reaches for the phone and examines the notification.

She opens the photo and notices Mark liked it.

Her eyebrows raise. Her head nods up and down.

She stares at herself in the bikini.

She opens Safari and searches:

"Where can I buy Ozempic in Melbourne 2026?"

END

12

"Shirts"

INT. THE SHOPPING CENTRE — DAY

Mark, our titular short, stocky, balding, Arab man, finds himself walking side-by-side with Lane in a busy shopping centre.

Their hands brush against each other. Mark retreats. Lane smirks, she holds his hand.

> LANE
>
> I think I'll buy you a shirt.

> MARK
>
> No thanks -

> LANE
>
> - You're meeting my friends, it's the least I can do.

> MARK
>
> I have too many shirts.

> LANE
>
> Please don't come out wearing another WWF -

> MARK
>
> - WWE -

> LANE
>
> - Like it matters Marky-Boy -

> MARK
>
> - I have buttons. I'll do buttons.

> LANE
>
> Come on! It'll be fun!

> MARK
>
> You and I have very different definitions of fun.

> LANE
>
> Maybe something black.

> MARK
>
> Yeah yeah, black is slimming.

>   LANE
> Well, black goes with everything.

>   MARK
> What I need new pants now?

>   LANE
> Why are you being like this?

Mark separates his hand from Lane's.

>   MARK
> I said no, and you keep pushing it, so I'm afraid I'll have to put
> my foot down.

Lane is confused by the sudden escalation.

>   LANE
> Fuck you, how's that?

Mark nods his head.

>   MARK
> Okay then. I'll see you.

Mark walks away. Lane exhales.

>   LANE
> Will you stop?

Mark stops. He turns around.

>   LANE
> Use your words.

>   MARK
> Don't condescend to me -- you see this is what --

>   LANE
> I didn't mean -

MARK

- I just didn't feel like being belittled today, yeah? Humiliated. Embarrassed. Not in front of you. In front of me, I can take it, I'm used to it, but I don't want to do it with an audience.

Beat.

LANE

What're you -

MARK

- Do you think someone like me can just go into any shop and buy a shirt? They don't make sizes for this! Whatever the fuck I am. I have to go to places called Mr Big or Deluxe Man or go to the fucking chemist or a parachute shop that repurposes old -- I can't just -- it's fucking embarrassing. So I wear American sized t-shirts. Whatever shirt fits.

Lane is stunned. Kind of ashamed. Mostly hurt, for Mark.

Beat.

LANE

Fuck.

Beat.

MARK

We gonna get a Big Mac or what?

Beat. Lane nods. She takes Mark's hand.

END

13
"Parking"

INT. MARK'S CAR — NIGHT

Mark, our titular short, stocky, balding, Arab man, sits behind the steering wheel, donning a snug, buttoned up shirt.

Lane, looking like a million bucks, sits in the passenger seat. She looks uneasy. One arm tightly clamped around the overhead hand rest.

They drive slowly through a full carpark.

MARK

Glen Waverley at 7PM on a Friday. Not the wisest idea.

Beads of sweat begin to form on his forehead.

LANE

It'll be fine. Syd's already inside.

MARK

I'm gonna walk in there, sweating bullets, late -- my first impressions are always nightmare fuel -

Mark notices a Man and a Woman walking slowly alongside the cars.

LANE

- You really are overthinking this -

MARK

- These casual strollers coming or going or what?

Mark rolls down the passenger side window.

Lane is visibly uncomfortable.

LANE

Don't --

Mark leans over and speaks to the Man and Woman through the window.

MARK

Hey -- Hi. Excuse me.

The Man and Woman stop.

MAN

Yeah?

MARK

Are you guys leaving?

Beat. The Man and Woman look at each other quizzically.

MAN

What?

Lane turns her head away.

MARK

Are you looking for your car?

The Man smirks at the Woman.

MARK
(to Lane)

What am I speaking Rotokas?

LANE
(quietly, confused)

What?

WOMAN
(to Man)

This guy's an asshole.

MAN
(dismissive)

No, we're not looking for our car.

The Man and Woman continue walking.

Mark shakes his head. He rolls up the passenger side window.

Mark and Lane continue driving slowly in the car park.

> LANE

Why'd you do that?

> MARK

What did I do?

> LANE

That was some spectacle.

> MARK

Spectacle? I asked a question.

> LANE

It was a bit much.

Beat. Mark scoffs.

Mark notices a car leaving.

> MARK

Found a spot.

Mark turns on the blinker.

> LANE

Yeah, great.

Lane exhales.

They sit in silence as they wait for the car to slowly reverse out and leave.

Mark pulls up to the space and positions himself to reverse in.

> LANE

What're you doing?

> MARK

Reversing in.

Lane smirks.

>   LANE
> You reverse park?

>   MARK
> Always.

Mark begins to reverse park the car.

He checks his mirrors. He stops reversing.

>   MARK
> Did you adjust your mirror?

>   LANE
> Did I what?

>   MARK
> I can't --

Mark starts adjusting the passenger side mirror.

Lane shakes her head.

Mark finishes adjusting the mirror and parks his car.

Lane immediately unbuckles her seatbelt.

Mark gently places his hand on Lane's. She stops.

>   MARK
> I'm just nervous.

Beat. Lane softens.

>   LANE
> Let's go.

Lane squeezes his hand and exits the car.

Mark rubs his face with his hands.

He wipes the sweat that's accumulated on his forehead.

He takes a breath.

He unbuckles his seatbelt and exits the car.

Beat.

END

14
"The Christmas Special"

4 MONTHS AGO

INT. CARIBBEAN GARDENS — DAY

Lane peruses the aisles at Caribbean Garden's crowded trash and treasure market.

A basket tucked under her left arm, leaving her right arm free to lift and examine any and all knick knacks, antiques or collectibles that catch her eye.

Vintage candle holders. Magazines from the 90s.

CDs. Cassettes. VHS tapes.

Action Figures. Pieces of furniture. Commemorative glasses.

When suddenly she spies a pristine pack of UNO cards sitting atop a stack of VHS tapes.

Her eyes light up.

She puts the basket down and examines the UNO cards.

The feel of the cardboard box. The crease along the fold of the pack.

She opens the pack and empties the cards into her hands.

She's transported back to her childhood when suddenly a familiar voice breaks the impending ecstasy:

> **MARK**
> Excuse me?
>
> *(louder)*
> Excuse me, miss?

Lane lifts her eyes to find our titular short, stocky, balding, Arab man, Mark, standing beside her.

> **LANE**
> Did you just call me miss?

> **MARK**
> Would you have preferred ma'am?

> **LANE**
> I would have preferred "Lane".

                              MARK
          Lane? Like the road?

                              LANE
          Sorry what do you want?

                              MARK
          Those are my UNO cards.

Lane grasps the UNO cards.

                              LANE
          I don't think so, buddy.

Mark tilts his head in confusion.

                              MARK
          Um, yeah it was on my pile. Do you see my pile?

Mark points at the pile of VHS tapes.

Lane puts the UNO cards back in their pack.

She examines the pile.

                              LANE
          This doesn't look like a claimed pile.

                              MARK
          What you think I'm making up piles?

                              LANE
          I think you're making up piles.

Beat. Mark looks at Lane. Really looks at her. Something in him softens.

                              MARK
          That's okay. You have it.

Mark scoops up his pile of VHS tapes.

A tinge of guilt quickly shoots through Lane.

                    LANE
          Sorry -- no of course this -

                    MARK
          - No problem. Have a good one.

Mark walks away.

Lane thinks for a beat. She isn't ready to conclude this interaction.

She calls after Mark.

                    LANE
          I'll play you for it.

Mark turns around. He's amused.

                    MARK
          What's that?

                    LANE
          One hand. Winner gets the pack.

                    MARK
          Really, it's okay. You don't have to -

                    LANE
          - Come on, I don't want to feel like shit over a pack of UNO
          cards.

Beat.

                    LANE
          At least this way there's no hard feelings.

Mark considers the offer.

INT. CARIBBEAN GARDENS — MOMENTS LATER

Mark and Lane pull up to a vintage dining room table.

They pull out a seat each and sit at the corner.

Mark's chair creaks.

MARK

I don't know if this chair is rated for public use.

Lane stifles a laugh.

LANE

You say things.

MARK

I do.

Lane opens the pack and begins shuffling.

LANE

Mind if I deal?

MARK

Sure.

Lane finishes shuffling the cards and begins dealing two hands.

LANE

What's your name?

MARK

Mark. Yours?

LANE

Lane.

MARK

Oh.

LANE

Like the road.

MARK

Apologies.

They pick up their cards.

Lane places a card face up in the middle.

They sort their cards, sneaking peeks at each other over their hands.

They both sit ready to play.

Mark places a card.

> **MARK**
> I haven't played UNO in a long time so --

Lane places her card. They alternate placing cards and picking them up from the draw pile.

> **LANE**
> Making excuses already?

> **MARK**
> I prefer it when expectations are exceptionally low. That's my sweet spot.

> **LANE**
> Strangely enough, I believe you.

They play.

> **MARK**
> Are you here with anyone?

Lane smirks.

> **MARK**
> No like, I mean, is someone going to be looking for you and then be outraged that you're making time with a moderately handsome Arab man?

> **LANE**
> You really do just say things.

Beads of sweat begin to form on Mark's forehead.

Lane notices.

LANE

Can't stand the heat, ey?

They are down to three cards each.

MARK

The stakes are high, what do you want?

LANE

No, I get it.

Quick beat.

LANE

I'm not here with anyone.

Mark places a card. He is left with one in his hand.

MARK

UNO. Both literally and figuratively.

LANE

Fuck.

Quick beat.

LANE

Oh.

Lane chuckles.

Lane places a card. She is left with one in her hand.

LANE

UNO. Here we go Marky Boy.

The card on the top of the discard pile is yellow.

Mark looks at his card. It's yellow.

He looks up at Lane. She smiles.

Instead of playing his winning card, Mark draws a card and holds it in his hand.

LANE
Oh! Too bad, mister!

Lane plays a yellow card. She wins.

Mark smiles. He puts his cards in the middle of the discard pile and begins to shuffle them.

LANE
Shuffling my cards too? What a gentleman.

They smile at one another.

Mark puts the cards in the box. He hands it to Lane.

MARK
Fair and square.

LANE
Fair and square.

Their smiles don't fade.

END

15
"Unshaken"

TODAY

INT. THE SUPERMARKET — NIGHT

Mark, our titular short, stocky, balding, Arab man, walks alongside, Lane, down the chips aisle.

They explore their options.

Doritos. Smiths. Toobz. Kettle. Red Rock Deli. Pringles.

Lane reaches for a tube of Salt & Vinegar Pringles.

She pops the plastic lid. Mark turns his head.

She peels the foil seal atop the tube.

Mark's eyes widen.

> **MARK**
> The fuck you doing?

Lane stops.

> **LANE**
> What?

Lane reaches for a chip.

> **MARK**
> Stop!

Lane stops. Smirks.

Mark speaks in hushed whispers. Makes sure no one can hear them.

> **LANE**
> What is your problem?

> **MARK**
> You can't just --

LANE
(egging him on)

I can't just --

MARK

Listen. I may be a lot of things -

LANE

- Yeah?

MARK

Yeah. I may be a lot of things, but I am not a shoplifter.

LANE

Who's shoplifting?

MARK

You're a criminal and I hope justice finds you.

Lane smirks. She reaches for a chip.

MARK

Close that fucking thing, will you?

Lane stops.

LANE

You really don't do this?

MARK

Grand larceny? No.

LANE

My family do this all the time. We grab a bag of chips to eat while we're shopping and just scan it during check out.

MARK

Anthony Woolworth let's us shop at his store and all he asks in return is that we don't steal. Eating a food item you've yet to pay for is theft.

LANE

I'm going to pay for it.

MARK

I'm sorry but the Supreme Court won't accept time travel
payment as a suitable defence.

LANE

Would you wait for me? If I got locked up?

MARK

Nah fuck that.

LANE
(feigning sadness)

Oh!

MARK

Your family does this?

LANE

All the time.

MARK

I'm dating the fucking Kelly gang.

Lane offers Mark a Pringle.

LANE

Go on.

MARK

Absolutely not.

LANE

You're such a fucking nerd.

MARK

Nerds run the world now, so, fuck you -- jock.

Lane smiles.

LANE

We'll pay for it first?

MARK

I have the money if that's what you're worried about.

LANE

I won't have to turn tricks?

MARK

Not yet.

She places the lid back on the tube. Tucks it under her arm.

LANE

Lead the way, Constable.

Mark offers Lane his arm. She links it.

LANE

Fucking nerd.

Mark chuckles.

END

www.ingramcontent.com/pod-product-compliance
Lightning Source LLC
Chambersburg PA
CBHW082246060726
47598CB00017B/2849